S0-AXA-074

# the coloring book of visual tricks & illusions

**This book belongs to:**

............................................

## STERLING CHILDREN'S BOOKS
New York

# Contents

## About this book

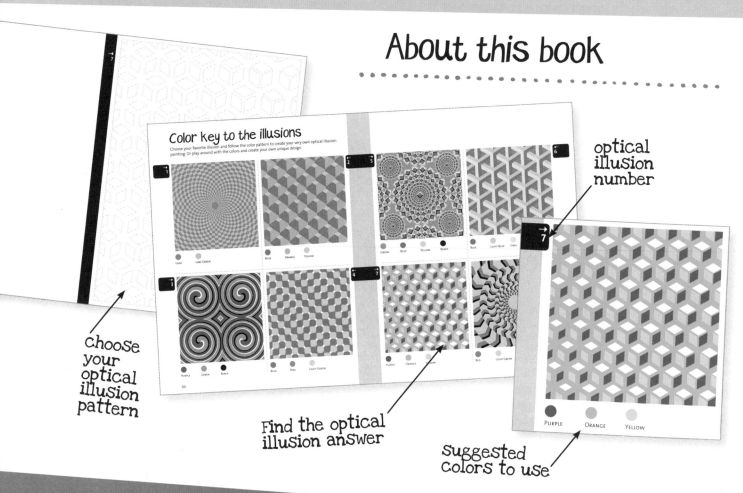

choose your optical illusion pattern

Find the optical illusion answer

optical illusion number

suggested colors to use

**STERLING CHILDREN'S BOOKS**
New York

An Imprint of Sterling Publishing Co., Inc.
1166 Avenue of the Americas

ISBN 978-1-4549-2565-1

Distributed in Canada by
Sterling Publishing Co., Inc.

c/o Canadian Manda Group,
664 Annette Street,
Toronto, Ontario,
Canada M6S 2C8

For information about custom
editions, special sales, and premium
and corporate purchases, please
contact Sterling Special Sales at
800-805-5489 or
specialsales@sterlingpublishing.com.

Manufactured in China
Lot #

2 4 6 8 10 9 7 5 3 1

12/16

www.sterlingpublishing.com

Copyright © 2017 by Quarto Inc.

All rights reserved. No part of this
publication may be reproduced,
stored in a retrieval system, or
transmitted in any form or by any
means (including electronic,
mechanical, photocopying, recording,
or otherwise) without prior written
permission from the publisher.

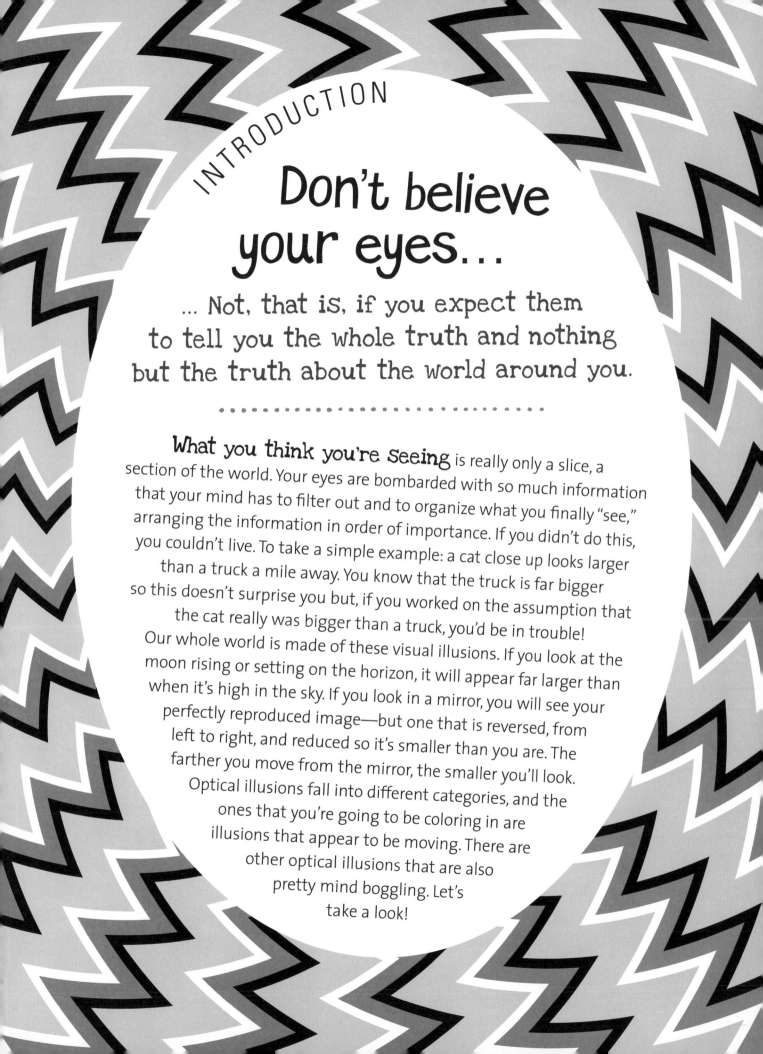

# Don't believe your eyes...

... Not, that is, if you expect them to tell you the whole truth and nothing but the truth about the world around you.

· · · · · · · · · · · · · · · · · · · · · · · · · · · · · · ·

**What you think you're seeing** is really only a slice, a section of the world. Your eyes are bombarded with so much information that your mind has to filter out and to organize what you finally "see," arranging the information in order of importance. If you didn't do this, you couldn't live. To take a simple example: a cat close up looks larger than a truck a mile away. You know that the truck is far bigger so this doesn't surprise you but, if you worked on the assumption that the cat really was bigger than a truck, you'd be in trouble! Our whole world is made of these visual illusions. If you look at the moon rising or setting on the horizon, it will appear far larger than when it's high in the sky. If you look in a mirror, you will see your perfectly reproduced image—but one that is reversed, from left to right, and reduced so it's smaller than you are. The farther you move from the mirror, the smaller you'll look. Optical illusions fall into different categories, and the ones that you're going to be coloring in are illusions that appear to be moving. There are other optical illusions that are also pretty mind boggling. Let's take a look!

# Optical confusions

Humans rely on eyesight to deal with the world. We tend to remember, recall, identify, and even dream in images. "I never forget a face," an older person might claim, while forgetting the name and everything else about who they are referring to. But when familiar objects are surrounded or crossed by totally unexpected and unusual patterns that simply don't occur in nature, the eye-brain partnership can be thrown into confusion, like a computer that's wrongly programmed.

## Snap judgement

Which line is longer? Make a guess, and then measure them against a ruler to see what is known as the Moller-Lyer effect in action. The line with the outward-pointing arrows seems to be much shorter than the other. In fact it's exactly the same length. This is just one example of our brain making a snap judgement that is just plain wrong.

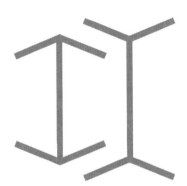

## Square deal

Which of these is as wide as it's tall? The two striped rectangles appear different. The horizontally striped shape on the right appears taller; the vertically striped shape on the left appears wider. In fact both are identical squares.

# Horizontals and verticals

People have used vertical and horizontal lines and stripes for centuries to decorate buildings, clothes, and even their bodies. But lines like these aren't always just decorative; sometimes they affect the way your eyes see objects, making them appear larger or smaller. Sometimes, even the simplest of intrusions into a shape can baffle the eye.

Generally, horizontal stripes make an area look higher while vertical stripes make it appear wider. Oddly, the effect isn't always obvious on people, as vertically striped clothes tend to make you look taller and thinner, while broad, horizontal stripes can make you look shorter and wider.

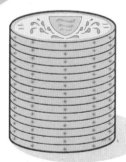

## ▲ Coin stacks

The stack on the right seems as high as it's broad. In fact, the stack on the left is equally wide and high, but the circular stripes around the coins fool the eye.

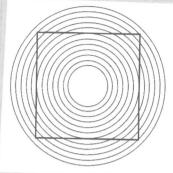

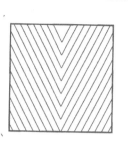
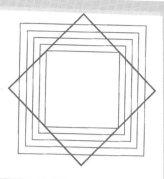

△ Is this square really bending inward?

△ An outward bulge?

△ Wider at the bottom?

△ Another inward-bending square?

## Bulgy squares

Few shapes appear more stable than a square. But squares can bulge and quiver as though they were made of jelly when strange patterns are superimposed on them. All these are illusions, for the squares are perfectly square.

## Defining shapes

If visual clues are added to the unclear images on this page, they become either a vase or two faces. If you want to see a vase, add a bouquet of flowers. If you'd prefer to look at two profiles facing each other, add a couple of appropriately placed eyes. It's amazing how such small touches can change the way we see a picture.

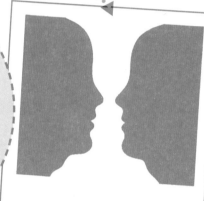

# Foreground and background

Glance at a simple drawing like the one on the right and you may see the white silhouette of a vase against a blue background. But if you blink or look away for a moment, the picture may suddenly become a pair of faces in profile, facing each other against a white background.

Edgar Rubin, the Danish psychologist who devised these images, said that what the brain tries to do is make a distinction between a shape in the foreground and a shapeless background. Rubin described this process as "reading" an image, for we "read" the external world in a way roughly similar to reading a book, making an instant distinction between the meaningful letters and the meaningless page. Understanding the real world requires us to interpret just as we must interpret letters to understand writing.

# The scientific approach

Scientists take an interest in tricks of the eye, and one of the earliest scientific demonstrations of optical ambiguity is the Necker Cube.

## where's the star?

As you look at the skeletal cube the star's position changes in front of your eyes. Is it at the front of the box, at the back, or in the middle?

## what can you see?

Do you see crimson or pink tools? Whichever you see, you can discover the total number of both on page 96.

# Adjusting to speed

Just as our eyes can be fooled by misleading signs in static images, so they can be fooled by movement. Some movement, like the shattering of a light bulb, is simply too fast for our eyes to register. Some, like the growing of a plant, is too slow. There are other movements that we see, but see wrongly, or in a particular way that creates optical illusions.

The Necker cube

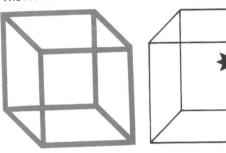 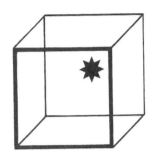 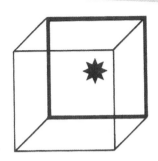

# Eyeball overload

Some artists have made art that baffles your eye and brain powerfully with their illusory movements. In the 1960s, the Op Art (short for Optical Art) movement began to experiment with pictures that stimulated the brain in such a way that they appeared to move. Check out the work of artists like Bridget Riley and Victor Vasarely who dazzled the eyes of the art world with startling geometric shapes. Vasarely's pictures seem to shift and change as you stare at them. Bridget Riley's pictures have an even weirder effect. Looking at them, your eye becomes totally bewildered, trying to read into them forms that are not actually there. Probably your retinal circuits are suffering a sort of overload. When you look away, your eyesight may flicker like a faulty television set.

## Mach's figure

One of the best examples of unclear images devised for scientific reasons is Ernst Mach's figure, the skeleton drawing of a half-open book. This could well be a book, your eye will tell you—but is the spine of the book thrust forward toward you? Or is the book open so that you're looking in to the spine, flanked by the open pages? It can be either, changing backward and forward in an eye-baffling instant.

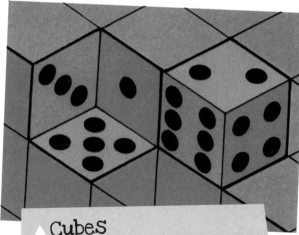

## ▲ Cubes

Concave or convex? Just when you think you know what you are seeing, the way you perceive the image alters.

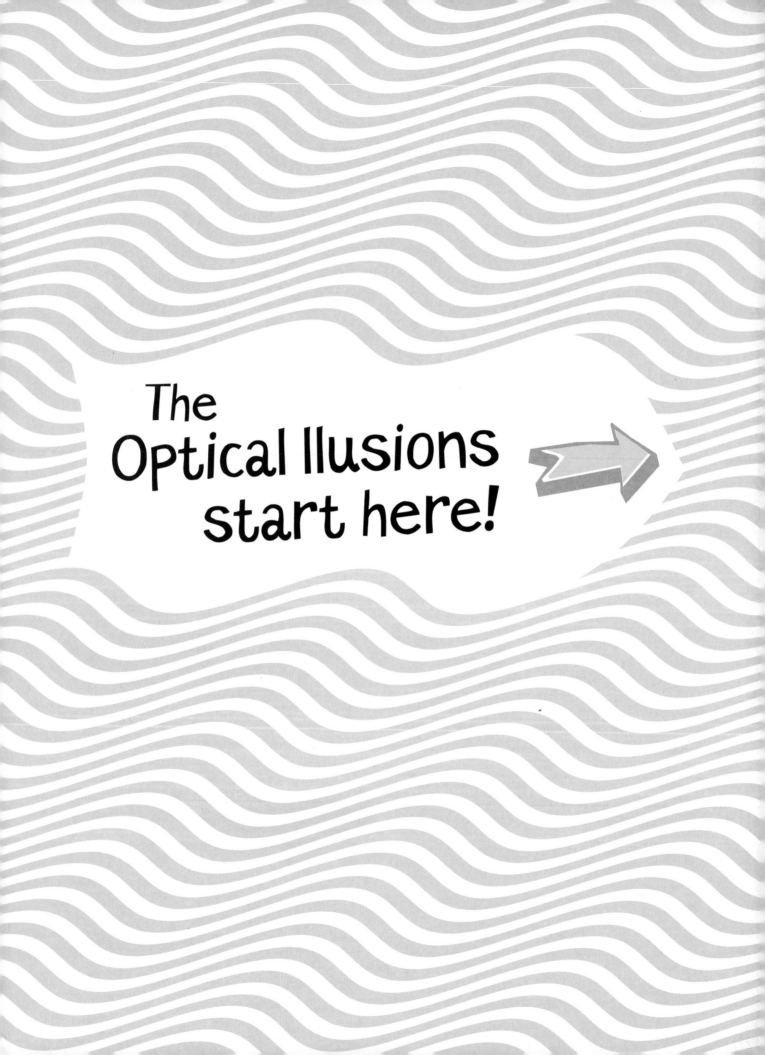

The
Optical Illusions
start here!

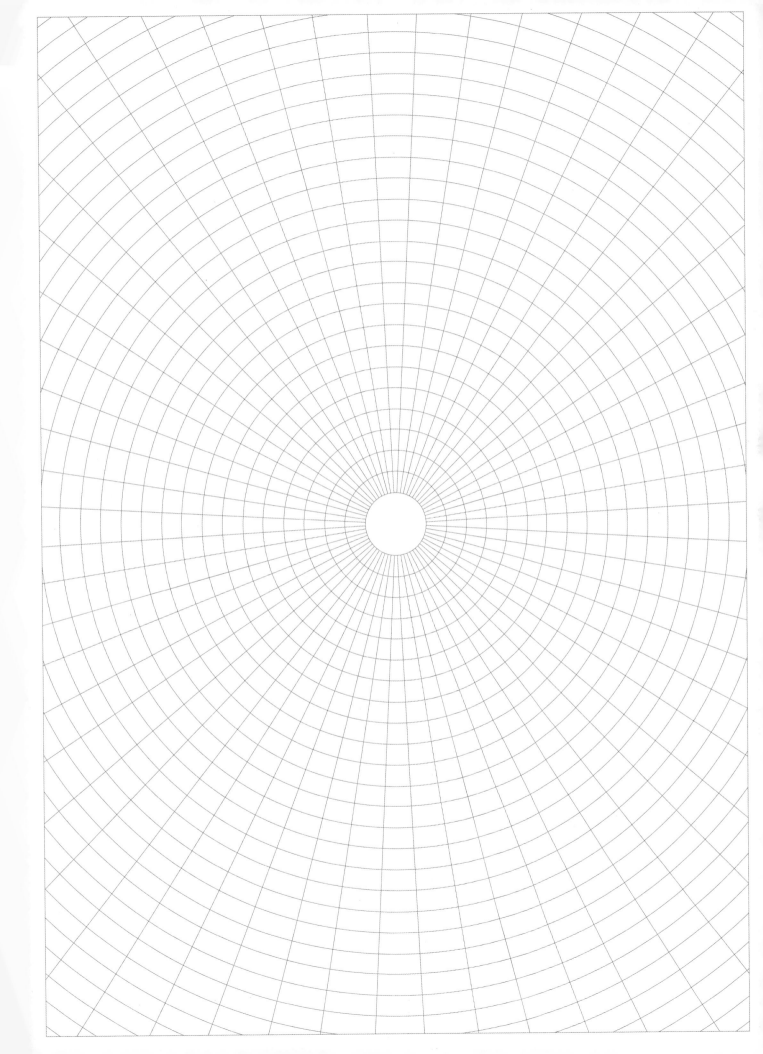

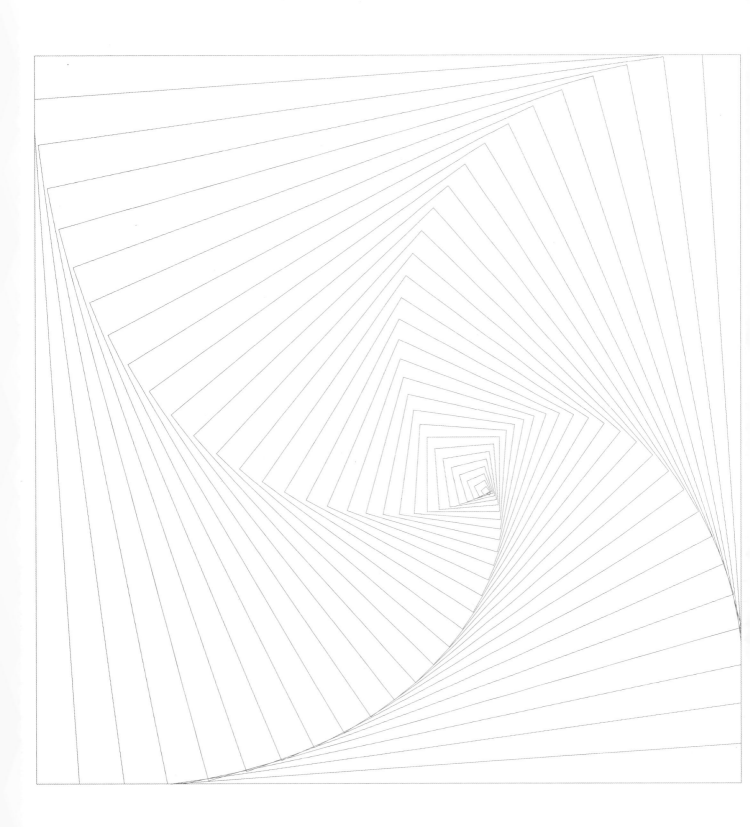

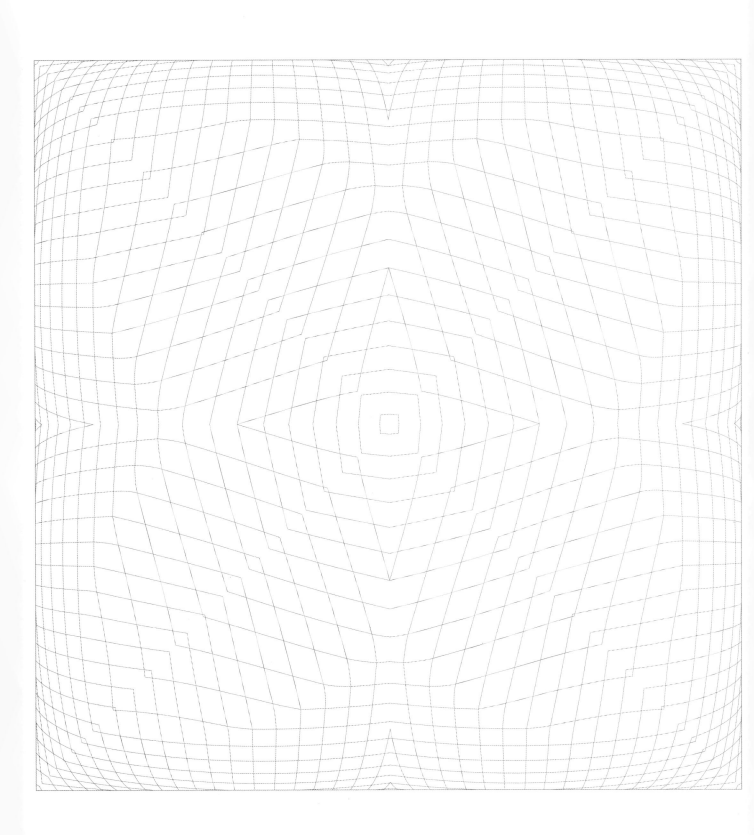

# Color key to the illusions

Choose your favorite illusion and follow the color pattern to create your very own optical illusion painting. Or play around with the colors and create your own unique design.

**1**

● LILAC  ● LIME GREEN

**2**

● BLUE  ● ORANGE  ● YELLOW

**3**

● PURPLE  ● GREEN  ● BLACK

**4**

● BLUE  ● PINK  ● LIGHT GREEN

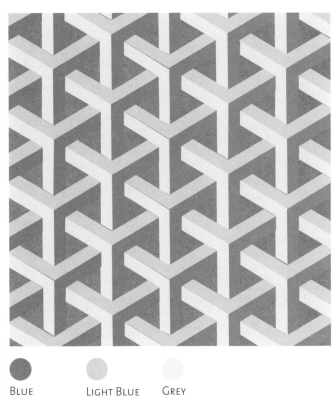

## 6

GREEN    BLUE    YELLOW    BLACK

BLUE    LIGHT BLUE    GREY

PURPLE    ORANGE    YELLOW

RED    LIGHT GREEN    YELLOW    BLACK

# Color key continued

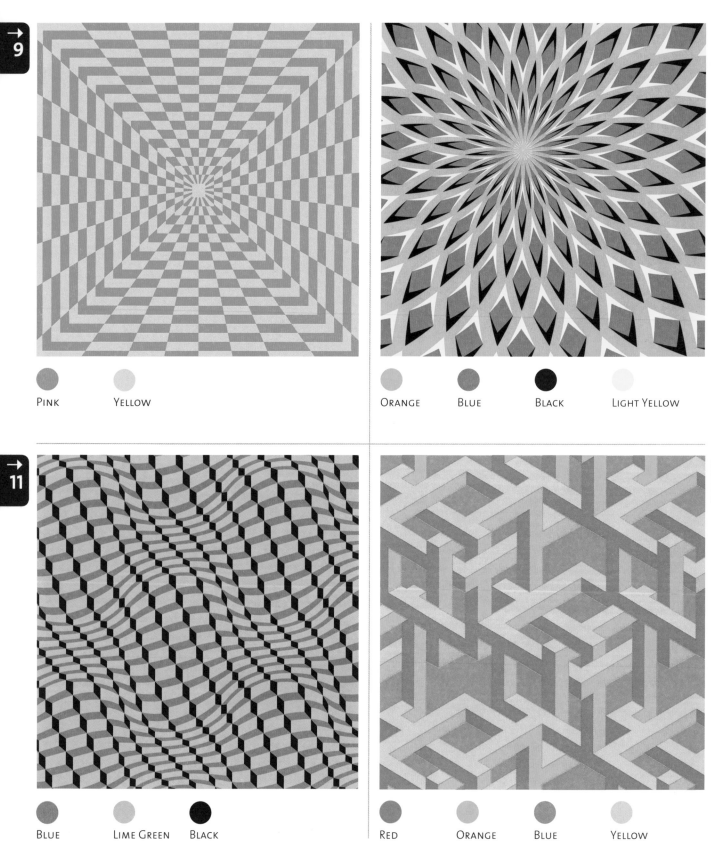

PINK  YELLOW

ORANGE  BLUE  BLACK  LIGHT YELLOW

BLUE  LIME GREEN  BLACK

RED  ORANGE  BLUE  YELLOW

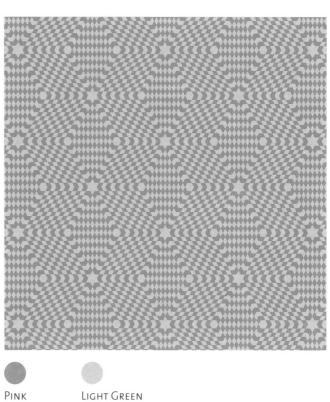

DARK GREEN   LIGHT ORANGE   LIGHT YELLOW

PINK   LIGHT GREEN

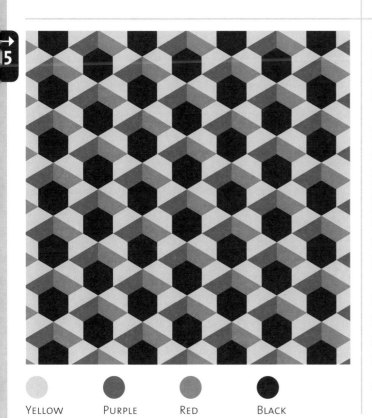

YELLOW   PURPLE   RED   BLACK

BLUE   GREEN

# Color key continued

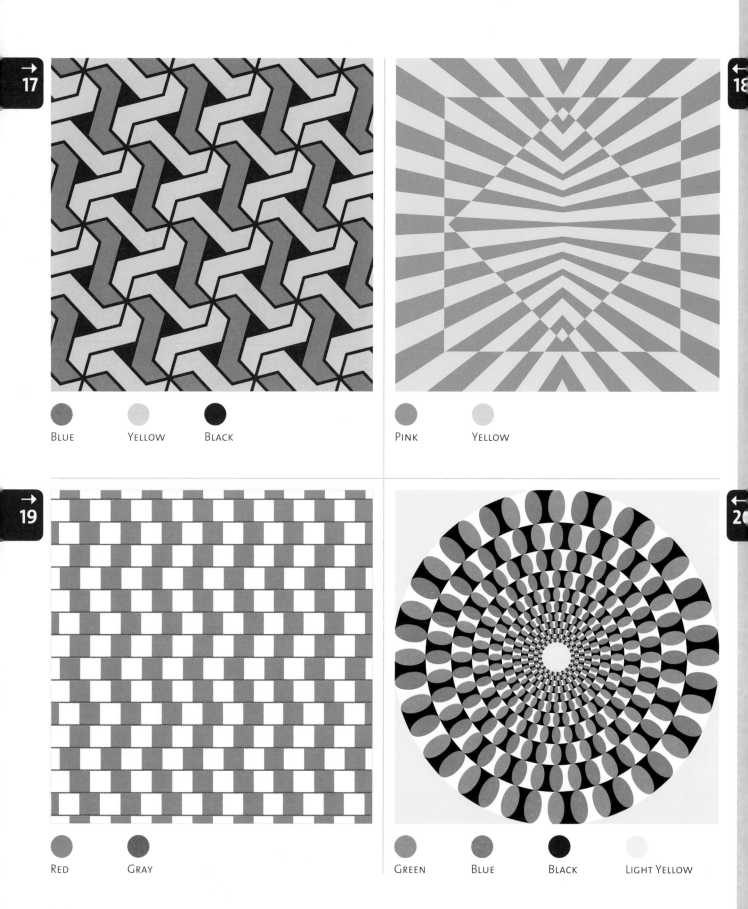

**17**

BLUE    YELLOW    BLACK

**18**

PINK    YELLOW

**19**

RED    GRAY

**20**

GREEN    BLUE    BLACK    LIGHT YELLOW

→ 21

← 22

LILAC        LIGHT BLUE

RED        YELLOW

→ 23

← 24

BLUE        YELLOW

AQUA        PURPLE        BLUE        GREEN

# Color key continued

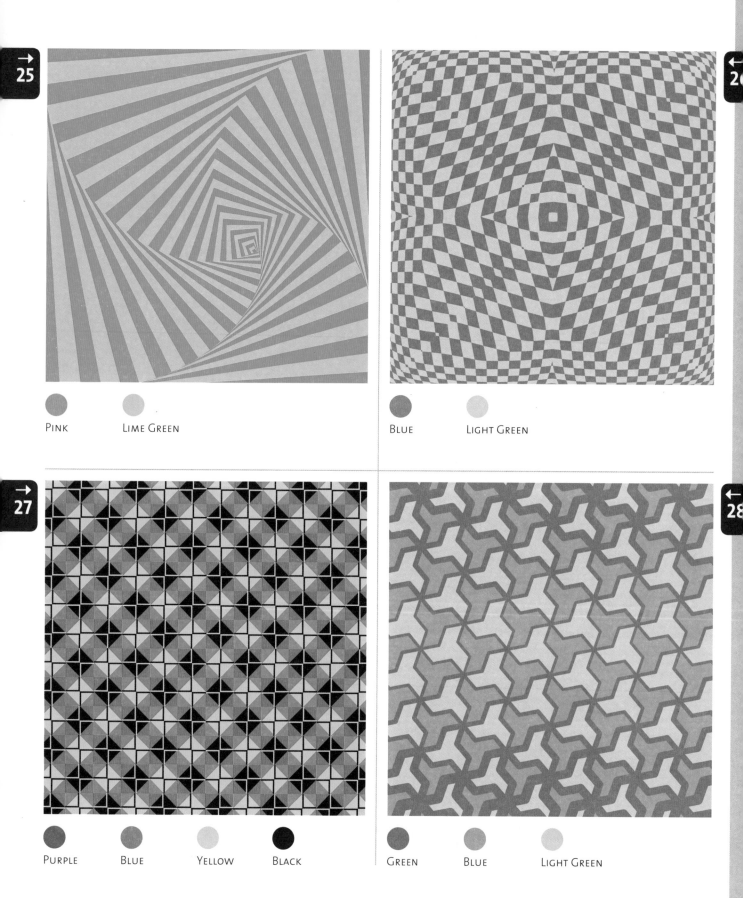

**25**

PINK    LIME GREEN

**2**

BLUE    LIGHT GREEN

**27**

PURPLE    BLUE    YELLOW    BLACK

**28**

GREEN    BLUE    LIGHT GREEN

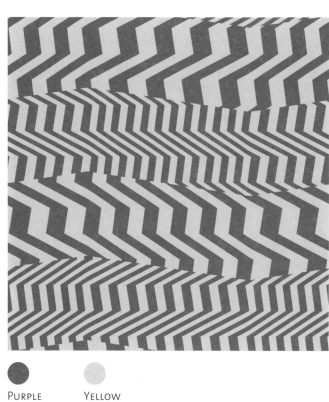

GREEN   RED   BLACK   LIGHT GREEN

PURPLE   YELLOW

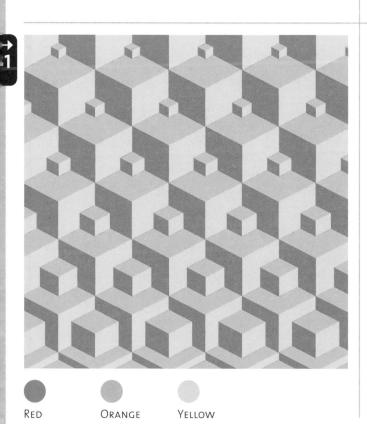

RED   ORANGE   YELLOW

BLUE   LIGHT YELLOW

# Color key continued

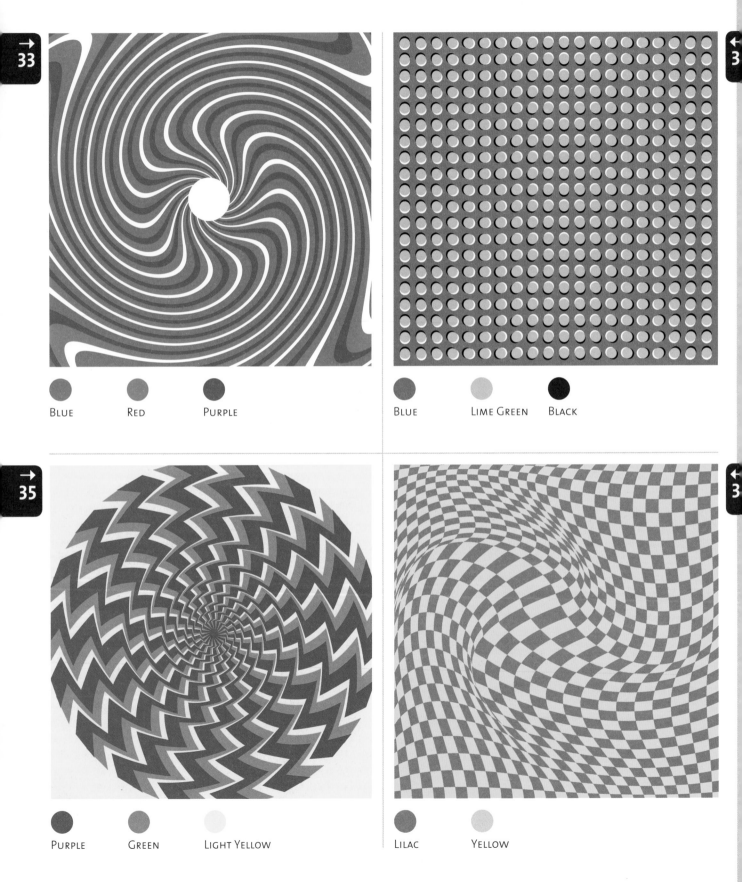

→ 33

BLUE   RED   PURPLE

← 3

BLUE   LIME GREEN   BLACK

→ 35

PURPLE   GREEN   LIGHT YELLOW

← 3

LILAC   YELLOW

● Red  ● Lime Green

● Purple  ● Green  ● Light Yellow  ● Black

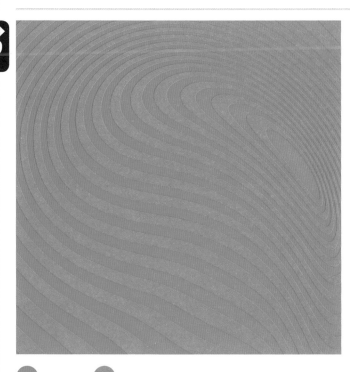

 ● Pink  ● Blue

 Dark Green   Light Green  ● Orange   Yellow   Black

# Credits

All images in the book are from the following sources:

Betacam-SP/Shutterstock.com, puzzles 4, 18, 23, 27, 32, 35
Cepera/Shutterstock.com, puzzles 16, 30
DEP, L./Shutterstock.com, puzzle 24
elfinadesign/Shutterstock.com, puzzles 15, 40
Elmiral/Shutterstock.com, puzzle 11
fat_fa_tin/Shutterstock.com, puzzle 31
Goldenarts/Shutterstock.com, puzzle 13
Grenier, Mark/Shutterstock.com, puzzles 10, 33, 38
HugoM/Shutterstock.com, puzzle 19
iconizer/Shuttertock.com, puzzle 7
irmairma/Shutterstock.com, puzzle 37
iro4ka/Shutterstock.com, puzzle 2
Korshenkov, Andrey/Shutterstock.com, puzzles 3, 29
Lychy/Shutterstock.com, puzzle 39
Oprea, Dana/Shutterstock.com, puzzle 36
Oxy_gen/Shutterstock.com, puzzle 25
pikepicture/Shutterstock.com, puzzle 8
Pinitspic/Shutterstock.com, puzzle 12
Samolevsky/Shutterstock.com, puzzles 6, 17, 28
ScottMurph/Shutterstock.com, puzzle 21
Shrivastava, Anjay/Shutterstock.com, puzzle 26
Shutterstock.com, puzzles 20, 34
Supermimicry/Shutterstock.com, puzzle 22
TanyaKalm/Shutterstock.com, puzzle 9
Tatiana, Skripnichenko/Shutterstock.com, puzzle 5
troyka/Shutterstock.com, puzzles 1, 14

Answer to puzzle on page 6:
There are 20 crimson and pink tools in total!